DECEMBER 24th

DENYS CAZET

BRADBURY PRESS   NEW YORK

Bradbury Press
An Affliate of Macmillan, Inc.
866 Third Avenue, New York, N.Y. 10022
Collier Macmillan Canada, Inc.
Printed and Bound in Japan.
2   4   6   8   10   9   7   5   3
The text of this book is set in 17 pt. Cheltenham Book.
The illustrations are drawn in ink with watercolor wash, reproduced in full color.

Library of Congress Cataloging-in-Publication Data

Cazet, Denys.
December 24th.

Summary: Young rabbits Emily and Louie have a special reason for giving their grandfather a present on December 24, but first he must guess why it's a special day.
[1. Rabbits—Fiction.   2. Grandfathers—Fiction.
3. Christmas—Fiction.   4. Birthdays—Fiction]   I. Title.
PZ7.C2985De   1986   [E]   86-8247
ISBN 0-02-717950-8

For Abel and Marie Carle

"Grandpa and Grandma!" Emily shouted. "We're here!"

"And we've got Grandpa's special present," said Louie.

"I'm in the kitchen," Grandma called. "Grandpa's in the living room."

"Surprise, Grandpa!" said Emily.

"A special present for a special day," said Louie.

"Well, thank you!" Grandpa said. "A Happy New Year's Day to you!"

"It's not a New Year's present," said Louie. "It's not even New Year's."

Grandpa smiled. "It's not?" he said.

"Can't you guess?" asked Emily.

"Of course I can guess," said Grandpa, standing up. "I know what holiday it is. I'll show you."

"Four score and two to nothing, our poor fathers brought forth a coconut . . ."

"No, Grandpa," said Louie. "It's not Lincoln's Birthday."

"It's not?" said Grandpa.

"Guess again," said Emily.

Grandpa disappeared into the bedroom.

"Look through the keyhole."
"I don't see him," said Emily.
"Listen," said Louie.

The doorbell rang.
"I got it!" Emily called.

"HAPPY VALENTINE'S DAY!"
shouted Grandpa.

"It's not Valentine's Day," said Emily.
"It's not?" said Grandpa.

"No, Grandpa," said Louie. "And it's not Washington's Birthday, either."

"Guess again," said Emily.

Grandpa danced back into the bedroom.

"Do you hear anything?" Emily asked.
"Shhh," said Louie.
"Shhh, yourself," said Emily.

"HAPPY EASTER!" shouted Grandpa.

"It's not time for the Easter Bunny," Louie said.

"And it's not the 4th of July, either," said Emily.

"It's not?" said Grandpa.

"Guess again," Emily said.

Grandpa hopped into the closet.

"It's very quiet in there," said Louie.
"Spooky quiet," Emily said.
"Something's moving," said Louie.

"HAPPY HALLOWEEEEEEEN,"
said a deep voice.
"Oh oh . . ."

"I am Count Rabbicula," said Grandpa.
"And the Count is very, very thirsty."

"Do you want a diet soda?" Emily asked.
"I want bunny blood," said the Count.
"RUN FOR YOUR LIFE!" shouted Louie.

"It's not Halloween, Grandpa."

"It's not?"

"No," said Louie. "And it's not Thanksgiving, either."

"You've got me woozled," Grandpa said. "I give up!"

"One more guess," said Emily. "We'll help you."

"Look," said Louie. "See the tree?"

"Remember, Grandpa?" Emily asked. "Everyone's socks—hung by the chimney with care?"

"Happy-You-Know-What-Day," said Louie.

"Ohhh!" said Grandpa. "I'll be right back."

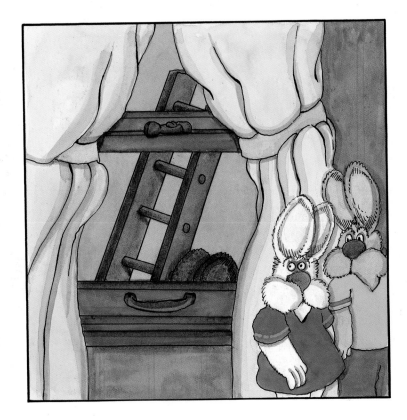

"Where did he go?" asked Louie.
"I don't know," Emily whispered.
"I hear something," said Louie.

"What is it?"
"It sounds like . . . sleigh bells," said Louie.
"Oh oh," said Emily.

"HO HO HO," said a jolly voice from the roof. "Whoa, Sneezy. Whoa, Dopey. Whoa, Big Belinda!"

"Grandpa!" shouted Emily. "Be careful!"
"I'm not Grandpa," said Grandpa. "Don't you
know Santa Claus when you hear him?"

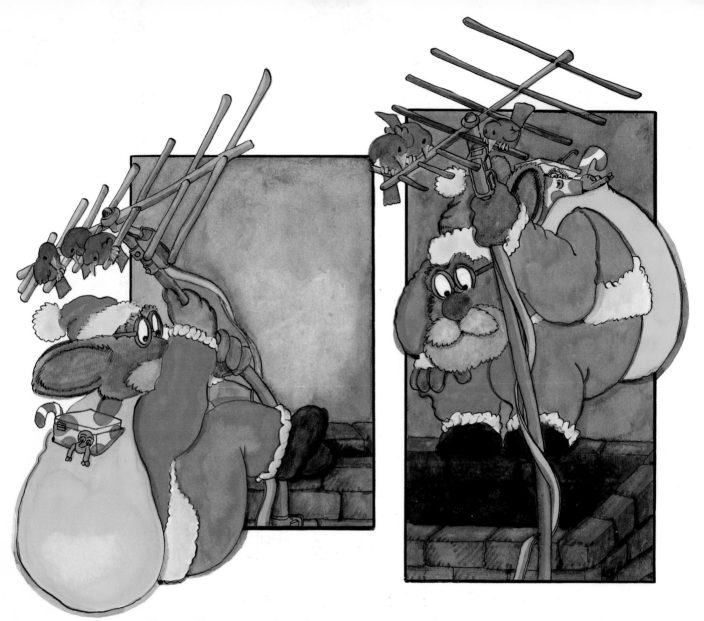

Grandpa climbed to the top of the chimney.

"Are all the good little boys and girls asleep in their beds?"

"Grandpa," said Louie, "it's two o'clock in the afternoon."

"What about naps?" Grandpa shouted.

Suddenly, the roof shook and the windows banged.

Ashes burst into the living room. Grandpa came rattling down the chimney.

Grandpa bounced out of the fireplace
and rolled onto the rug.

"Mercy sakes!" cried Grandma. "Are
you all right?"

Grandpa smiled. "Happy Christmas," he said.
"Grandpa," said Louie, "*tomorrow* is Christmas."
Emily handed Grandpa his present.

"Happy Birthday, Grandpa."